Dear mouse friends,
Welcome to the world of

Geronimo Stilton

THE RODENT'S GAZETTE
EDITORIAL STAFF

Geronimo Stilton
A learned and brainy
mouse; editor of
The Rodent's Gazette

Thea Stilton
Geronimo's sister and
special correspondent at
The Rodent's Gazette

Trap Stilton
An awful joker;
Geronimo's cousin and
owner of the store
Cheap Junk for Less

Benjamin Stilton
A sweet and loving
nine-year-old mouse;
Geronimo's favorite
nephew

Geronimo Stilton

THE MYSTERY IN VENICE

Scholastic Inc.

New York   Toronto   London   Auckland
Sydney   Mexico City   New Delhi   Hong Kong

ISBN 978-0-545-34097-7

Copyright © 2009 by Edizioni Piemme S.p.A., Via Tiziano 32, 20145 Milan, Italy.

International Rights © Atlantyca S.p.A.

English translation © 2012 by Atlantyca S.p.A.

Based on an original idea by Elisabetta Dami.
www.geronimostilton.com

Published by Scholastic Inc., 557 Broadway, New York, NY 10012.
SCHOLASTIC and associated logos are trademarks and/or registered trademarks of Scholastic Inc.

Stilton is the name of a famous English cheese. It is a registered trademark of the Stilton Cheese Makers' Association. For more information, go to www.stiltoncheese.com.

Text by Geronimo Stilton
Original title *Il mistero della gondola di cristallo*
Cover by Giuseppe Ferrario
Illustrations by Lorenzo De Pretto (pencils) and Davide Corsi (color)
Graphics by Yuko Egusa

Special thanks to Kathryn Cristaldi
Translated by Julia Heim
Interior design by Kay Petronio

12 11 10 9 8 7 6 5   12 13 14 15 16 17/0

Printed in the U.S.A.   40
First printing, January 2012

I'm Dragging from Jet Lag

It was a *hot* summer day and I was exhausted. I had just returned from a trip to the Restful Tails Resort in the Swiss Alps and I was dragging from jet lag.

So much for feeling restful! I could barely keep my eyes **open**!

I'm exhausted!

Don't get me wrong — I love visiting Switzerland. I mean, who wouldn't love the place where they invented Swiss cheese? But flying back and forth between time zones had left me with a terrible case of jet lag.

Do you know what JET LAG is?

It's something that happens to rodents when they travel by plane and cross from one time zone into another. Your body clock feels like it's one time, but the local clock says it's another. It makes your insides feel like curdled cheese!

First your head gets **heavy**, then your eyes begin to **close**,

TIME ZONES

The Earth is divided into twenty-four sections called time zones.

Every section corresponds to an hour. When you travel across continents, your watch must be adjusted an hour for every section you cross. If you go east, the hour is added, and if you go west, the hour is subtracted. So if it is eight p.m. in London, it is three p.m. in New York.

then your stomach gets **upset**, and then your tail **droops**. Plus, the worst part is that at night, your body thinks it's still morning, so you can't fall asleep!

Cheese niblets! I hate jet lag!

This is one of the many reasons that I have never loved to travel. In fact, I guess you could say my two most favorite places in the world are my cozy **mouse hole** and my office at *The Rodent's Gazette.*

Oh, how rude. I haven't even introduced myself. My name is Stilton, *Geronimo Stilton,* and I am the publisher of *The Rodent's Gazette,* the most famous newspaper on Mouse Island.

Anyway, what was I saying?

Ah, yes, I was telling you how much **I WAS DRAGGING FROM JET LAG**!

But luckily I had a plan.

I was going to put my anti–jet lag remedy into action: a warm bath, pajamas, slippers, a cup of tea, and right to bed!

But as soon as I started to relax, the telephone rang.

I got out of the tub grumbling. ❶ First, I couldn't find my bath towel, so I grabbed one that was way too small. ❷ Next, I headed toward the living room dripping soapy water everywhere. Meanwhile, the telephone

kept ringing and ringing. Rats! It was giving me a **mouse-sized headache!** ③ As I raced for the phone, I slipped on a puddle and fell on my tail. ***Ouch!*** ④ I tried to get up but lost my balance and fell forward right on my snout. **THUMP!** ⑤ Finally, I reached the phone and stammered,

"H-h-hello?"

Thump!

H-h-hello?

THE RODENT
OF MY DREAMS!

From the other end of the line, a sweet voice responded, "Hi, G, you sound funny. Am I bothering you?"

It was Petunia Pretty Paws, *the rodent of my dreams*!

I should have said something clever, charming, and unforgettable.

Instead, I turned **purple** with embarrassment (good thing I don't have a videophone), my tongue felt like a stale **BRICK** of cheddar, and I spit out silly sentences.

"Yes—I mean no. That is, what I mean is . . . I am

Umm...

Geronimo and you no **disturb** me. I mean, you're not . . . You would never, that is—"

She interrupted me, sounding worried. "Are you sure you're feeling **all right?**"

I touched the bump on my head. Then I rubbed the bruise on my tail and felt my whiskers droop. "I have **JET LAG**, a **bruised tail**, and a terrible **headache**!" I wailed.

She was silent for a minute. "Oh, too bad," she said kindly. "I wanted to invite you—"

At that moment my spirits **soared**. "Okay, I'll come! I'm feeling better already!" I squeaked. There was no way I was going to miss spending time with Petunia.

"Great! I'll be by to get you in ten minutes," she replied.

I hung up the phone and smiled. Yes, I still felt AWFUL from the jet lag. My head was **pounding**. My stomach hurt. But I didn't care. I was too *HAPPY*! Petunia had invited me to go out with her! My heart was **BEATING** a mile a minute and I began to skip around the room, shouting HOORAY!

Then, **SUDDENLY**, I realized that I hadn't asked her where she wanted to invite me. . . .

I chewed my whiskers. How was I supposed to dress?

A Elegant and sophisticated?

B Sporty and casual?

C Normal, like every day?

With my mind racing, I began to try on all different combinations of clothes at **warp speed**. Soon shirts and pants and ties and socks littered the room . . . but nothing looked good!

Right at that moment, the doorbell rang: Ding-dong!

I was so excited I ran to open the door without thinking about how I was dressed.

Ruffled yellow dress shirt

The usual green suit jacket

Bermuda shorts

Mouse slippers

DING-DONG!

I opened the door with a charming smile, but in just a few seconds my face went from **happy** to **shocked** to em*barrassed* to **crushed**.

Do you want to know why?

It was because as soon as I opened the door, I saw that Petunia wasn't alone. She was with my sister, THEA, and Petunia's pesky niece, Bugsy Wugsy.

HAPPY GERONIMO

SHOCKED GERONIMO

EMBARRASSED GERONIMO

CRUSHED GERONIMO

Good-bye romantic stroll and candlelit dinner!

At that moment, Bugsy looked me up and down and shrieked, "Uncle G, why are you dressed like a CLOWN?"

DISAPPOINTED GERONIMO

Only then did I remember that I was dressed in a ridiculous outfit. I turned PURPLE.

"Oh, ha-ha, I was just kidding around. I'll just go change . . ." I mumbled, trying to laugh it off. But before I got a chance, Thea grabbed me and pulled me out of the house.

"No time, Ger!" she squeaked. "The early mouse gets the best bargains!"

Petunia added, "She's right, G! The best pieces DISAPPEAR in a hurry. . . ."

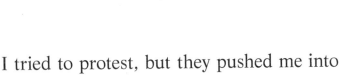

I tried to protest, but they pushed me into Thea's **sports car**, shouting, "Hurry, we need to go!"

"Can I at least know where we're going?" I asked.

"To the flea market." Bugsy giggled. Then the three of them screamed:

"WE'RE GOING SHOPPING!!!"

Long live shopping!

At that point my spirits took a nosedive. Flea market? Shopping?

Oh, why, why, why hadn't I stayed home?

If there's one thing I hate almost as much as traveling, it's **shopping**! But before I had time to protest, Thea's car screeched to a halt and Bugsy screamed in my ear, "Move it, Uncle G, we're here!"

We had arrived at the **New Mouse City Flea Market**. Have you ever been to a flea market? It's not a place where they sell fleas. It's a market where they sell trinkets, used clothing, old dishes, pictures, and lots of other junk.

A SURPRISE GIFT!

As soon as we arrived, Bugsy, Thea, and Petunia immediately began to browse the stands with **ENTHUSIASM**. I, on the other paw, felt like I would **EXPLODE FROM BOREDOM**! What was so exciting about other rodents' junk?

I tried closing my eyes and pretending I was back home in my cozy mouse hole, but it didn't work. As I plodded glumly through the market, I could hear everyone **chuckling** about how I was dressed.

"What's with the **slippers**?"

"How **BIZARRE**!"

"Who is that **ridiculous** mouse?"

How humiliating!

I turned **PURPLE** with embarrassment.

Quickly, I grabbed a hat from a rack and

shoved it on my head, hoping that no one would recognize me. Unfortunately, the elderly rodent behind the stand thought I was stealing it and began whacking me with her umbrella.

"**Thief!**" she screamed.

To get her to stop, I tore the hat off my head, at which point she recognized me.

"Aren't you *Geronimo Stilton,* the famouse writer?" she shouted.

"No, ma'am, I'm just a rodent who looks a lot like him," I **squeaked**.

That made her even angrier.

Thief!

"How dare you make fun of me? I recognize you! You are Stilton or my name's not **Mildred Pawnette Busybody!**" she shrieked.

Then she whacked me again with her umbrella. Youch! **STARS** swam before my eyes.

Oh, why, why, why hadn't I stayed home?

Finally, the old lady stopped hitting me and I told her I was doing research for my next book and was trying to keep a low profile. Then, to be sure she would leave me alone, I began to carefully examine the merchandise at the first stand I came across. It was a stand that sold **CRYSTAL GONDOLAS**. Do you know what a gondola is? It is a boat mice use to travel around the canals in the city of *Venice, Italy.*

I picked one up and stared at it closely, turning it over and over in my paws. *What a hideous piece of junk*, I thought.

As I mentioned, the gondola was made of crystal, with **COLORED STONES** and fake diamonds on the prow. If you clapped your paws, lights blinked on and off and a silly song began to play:

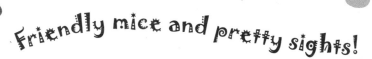

Venice is the place for you.

Pizza pies and skies of blue!

Tasty treats and starry nights.

Friendly mice and pretty sights!

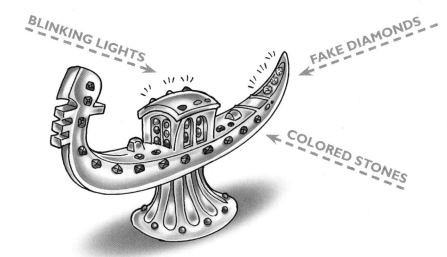

BLINKING LIGHTS

FAKE DIAMONDS

COLORED STONES

When I was sure the old lady had left, I put the u g l y gondola back.

Three torturous hours later, when we were ready to leave, Petunia approached me.

She gave me a kiss on the whiskers and handed me a package.

"This is for you, G," she said. "I wanted to apologize for *dragging* you out shopping."

I unwrapped the package and found . . . **the hideous gondola!**

Petunia smiled. "I'm not sure why you like

it, but I saw you staring at it, so I bought it for you," she explained.

What could I say? I didn't have the courage to tell her that the glittering gondola was the **ugliest** thing I'd ever laid eyes on.

So I just mumbled, "Thanks!"

A MYSTERIOUS
CALL FOR HELP

We climbed back into Thea's sports car and headed for home. As we drove, the crystal gondola kept **lighting up** and playing its annoying song. The music was so **LOUD**, mice on the streets shot me disgusted looks as we passed by.

How humiliating!

When we arrived at my mouse hole, I said good-bye and ran inside. I couldn't wait to get out of my *ridiculous* outfit and put on my regular clothes.

After I got changed, I looked around for somewhere to put the gondola. Since it was a **gift** from Petunia, I couldn't hide it in the back of a drawer somewhere, or under the bed, or in a closet. I needed to leave it in plain sight. I started wandering around the house, looking for the perfect spot.

Umm . . . on the mantel?

No, it wouldn't fit.

On the COFFEE TABLE?

No, it clashed with the carpet.

On the nightstand?

No, if that annoying song went off, I'd never get to sleep.

Right at that moment the doorbell rang. I ran to open it, but the door burst open and I was **KNOCKED** over by my cousin Trap. The crystal gondola fell to the floor, breaking into a thousand pieces.

I tried to put the pieces back together as tears fell from my eyes. Even though the gondola was hideous, it was a **gift** from Petunia! I was devastated!

"Trap, how could you!" I wailed. "That was a present from **Petunia**!"

"What's the big deal?" Trap chuckled. "It's

Oh, no! Oh, no!

What's the big deal?

not like she's your girlfriend or anything."

I GLARED at him. My cousin knows that I have a crush on Petunia and I am too shy to tell her. Of course, that doesn't stop him from teasing me about it.

"She bought me that CRYSTAL GONDOLA at the flea market today," I squeaked. "Now that you broke it, she'll think I didn't like it. I'll never be able to tell her I like her, and it's all your fault!"

He giggled. "You should thank me, Cousin!" he replied. "From the little that is left, I can really tell that thing was hideous!"

But it was hideous!

I ignored him and started picking up TINY pieces of crystal in hopes of fixing the gondola.

It was then that I realized that

a piece of **rolled~up** paper had been stuck inside the gondola. I unrolled it and read these words:

I gulped. It was a dramatic call for help. I had to do something **immediately**!

"Look at this!" I squeaked, shoving the paper under my cousin's nose. "Someone is in **DANGER** and needs help! Maybe it's a damsel in distress!"

Trap just rolled his eyes. "You'll never change, Germeister. How many times do

I have to tell you to get your head out of those adventure books? You imagine you see **damsels** that need saving everywhere. Just wait, I'm going to tell your *almost* girlfriend! Geronimo thinks he's A KNIGHT IN SHINING ARMOR!"

Then he left in a **hurry** to go and blab it all to Petunia.

DESTINATION: VENICE!

I tried to grab Trap's tail as he ran off, but he managed to slip away. **RATS!** Who knew what he would say to Petunia!

Maybe he'd say I was **SMASHING** her crystal gondola to bits. Or maybe he'd say I was running around pretending to be a knight in SHINING armor. Either way, I'd never have a chance with her now!

Still, there was no time to worry about it. Someone out there needed my **HELP**, and I was just the mouse for the job!

After all, I may not be the bravest mouse on the block, but I am a true gentlemouse. If someone needed *assistance*, I had to take action.

With a sigh, I picked up the **mysterious paper** and began to examine it very carefully.

Who knows how long it had been inside the gondola! The writing was very neat and the dots on the exclamation points were in the shape of **hearts**, which made me think the author was female. Plus, the paper was scented.

Right at that moment I noticed a small tag attached to what remained of the crystal gondola.

It was a certificate of authenticity. It said *Authentic Murano Crystal.*

So the gondola had been made in *Italy,* on the island of Murano in Venice!

Before you could say **Squeak**, I had packed my bags. I went to the airport and boarded a flight to *Venice.*

I didn't say anything to anyone.

What would I have said?

That I was leaving to solve a **mystery in Venice**? That I was going to save a damsel who *maybe* needed help?

I knew it seemed absurd. Everyone would laugh at me.

As soon as I boarded the plane, I fell asleep.

I woke up only when the plane was landing at the airport in Venice. That's when a voice next to me squeaked,

"wake up, my precious fuzzy fur.... we've arrived!"

I opened my eyes and realized that I had fallen asleep with my head resting on the shoulder of a **STRANGE** lady mouse!

I jumped up, **purple** from embarrassment. "I-I-I'm s-s-so sorry," I stammered.

She smiled at me, batting her **BIG**, extremely made-up eyes. Her **LONG** fake eyelashes nearly slapped me in the snout.

"Don't worry your handsome little self.

How about we do some sightseeing together in Venice, my precious DARLING?" she crooned.

My fur turned RED. I mumbled something about having a lot of things to do, but she didn't take the hint.

"You have things to do?" she squeaked. "So you mean you're not here on vacation? You actually live in Venice?! **How romantic!** I knew that I would find the mouse of my dreams on my trip to Venice!"

I gulped. This mouse was starting to scare me. I backed slowly away from her, then turned on my tail and took off at *breakneck speed.*

"I'm not from Venice!" I yelled over my shoulder. "You misunderstood me!"

She followed me, but I lost her in the crowd.

When I arrived at the water taxi stand, however, I saw her pink spotted hat in the crowd. *How had she followed me?*

I made a quick about-face, but she had seen me.

"Why are you **RUNNING**?" she yelled. "Why are you abandoning me, my sweet little Venetian mouse?"

What could I do? I started running again. **"I'm not from Venice!"** I shouted back at her.

All the rodents in the taxi line looked at me with disgust.

They started talking about me.

"What a **heartless** rodent!"

"Who leaves his girlfriend like that?"

"He's no **gentlemouse!**"

I would have loved to defend myself. I pride myself on my reputation as a true gentlemouse. But there was no time. I had a mission to accomplish. I had to solve the **mystery in Venice!**

I didn't have time to deal with a clingy lady mouse in a polka-dot hat! I ran down the dock with my paws in the air.

THE RODENT OF MY NIGHTMARES!

I scanned the water for an available motorboat taxi and jumped on the first one I came to. The driver, a guy with huge **MUSCLES** and a black mustache, asked, "Where would you like to go, sir?"

"Wherever you want, just as long as it's FAR AWAY from here!" I squeaked, hoping the clingy lady mouse was still way behind me.

The driver took off and headed toward the city. Only when we were safely splashing through the open water did I turn to admire the Grand Canal.

The Grand Canal

A little over two miles long, the Grand Canal is the main waterway in Venice. It divides the historic center into two parts. Along this canal, you can find magnificent buildings that were constructed between the twelfth and eighteenth centuries. It is also the place where the Venetians celebrate the Historic Regatta (see page 98).

What a fabumouse sight!

Just then a steamboat filled with tourists taking pictures pulled up next to us. Among them I recognized a familiar pink polka-dot hat. . . . IT WAS HER! THE RODENT OF MY NIGHTMARES!

I groaned. I had to do something. Then I got an idea. I asked the driver if he would sell me his hat so I could disguise myself. The driver's eyes lit up. I guess he could tell I was desperate.

"How much are you willing to pay?" he asked.

I gave him EVERYTHING I had in my wallet, but he wanted my GOLD watch, too!

Finally, I put on the hat. It didn't work. My admirer recognized me anyway. She shouted at me from the steamboat,

"Oh, Fuzzy Fur, why are you running away from me? I am your true love! Come back!"

Venice

Venice is a unique city because it is built entirely on water. It extends along 120 separate islands divided by canals but connected by more than four hundred bridges.

Venice is one of the most fascinating cities in the world for art lovers. Bell towers, churches rich with works of art, antique buildings with finely decorated facades, and houses with mysterious courtyards all face onto the lagoon. On the inside, the city is a labyrinth of streets, small squares, and small covered passages that make it even more mysterious.

In Venice you can't get around by bus or by car. Instead, people travel by steamboats, motorboats, or gondolas, which are typical Venetian rowboats.

HELP, I'M
DROWNING!

Suddenly, the taxi driver grabbed me by the tail and TOSSED me into the Grand Canal.

"That'll teach you to mistreat your **true love**!" he squeaked.

"But wait—I can explain!" I wailed. "It's all a **misunderstanding**!"

Darling!

HELP!

I could hear the mouse in the polka-dot hat shouting from the steamship, "Save him! I don't want him to **DROWN**! I want to marry him!"

Someone threw a buoy made of cork into the water and it hit me right in the head. What a **BLOW**!

So much for a **rescue**! I think they did it on purpose.

In fact, someone from the steamboat yelled, "What kind of **ROTTEN** rat treats a lady mouse like that? He should be left out to sea!"

At that point I didn't have a choice. I began to sink. I swam underwater, holding my breath until I reached a secondary canal that smelled of rotten fish!

Yuck, what a terrible stench!

But what could I do? I hid under a bridge

until evening, to be sure that my clingy admirer was long gone.

While I was hiding, I began to HICCuP. I hoped no one would hear me. Oh, how had I gotten myself into this mESS?

I sighed loudly, full of pity for myself. SIGH! SIGH! SIGH!

Suddenly, a voice up on the bridge squeaked, "Did you hear that? Someone is sighing!"

"Of course. We're standing on the Bridge of Sighs," another voice said.

"Maybe it's a ghost!" a third voice shrieked.

Then I heard paws scampering overhead. Quietly, I slipped out of the water.

I stood on the dock

and sighed for the millionth time that night. What a **fiasco**! I had been so busy running away from my lady admirer I hadn't even begun to solve the **mystery in Venice**.

I took a deep breath and resolved to get moving. I would start looking for clues right away, even though I was soaking wet, **freezing**, and above all, **stinking** of rotten fish!

I tried not to think about the stench as a cloud of **flies** followed me down the narrow streets of Venice. By this time it was pretty late in the evening and the whole city seemed deserted.

That was actually a good thing, since I felt like I was playing the starring role in the horror movie **Mouse Monster of the Lagoon**!

I slunk along, whiskers drooping, leaving PUDDLES behind me. The few tourists I encountered made sure to keep far away from me, covering their snouts with their paws. Oh, how humiliating!

I was still feeling sorry for myself when I entered Piazza San Marco. In an instant, I forgot all about my troubles as I stared at the gorgeous antique buildings, the marvelous cathedral with four domes, the BRONZE horses, and the TALL bell tower. What an amazing place!

Right then a flock of rude pigeons sailed overhead, dropping small GIFTS on my head, my back, and my tail. . . . Oh, how humiliating!

Shoo! Shoo!

HELP, THE MONSTER OF THE LAGOON!

At that point I decided I had to clean myself up. I was sticky and **slimy**, and my stomach was growling up a storm. I was **starving**!

Lucky for me, just then I spotted a café still open in the square. I made my way to one of the *elegant* outside tables. BIG MISTAKE!

Just as I arrived, I saw her little pink polka-dot hat and her fake eyelashes. . . . It was the rodent of my **NIGHTMARES**!

As soon as she spotted me, she yelled, "**OOOOOH!**"

The rodent next to her shrieked, "**Eeeeeeh!**"

The waiter by the door shouted, **"Aaaaaah!"**

Then there were the sounds of breaking glass, clanging silverware, and shattering trays. And before I knew it, everyone ran off screaming,

"HELP! IT'S THE MOUSE MONSTER OF THE LAGOON!"

I looked around in a panic. **MONSTER?** Could there really be a monster on the loose? My heart began **hammering** as fast as the drummer who plays on the new Wild Whiskers CD, *Cheddar's Burning*.

I entered the deserted café on shaky paws and quickly hightailed it to the bathroom to get cleaned up. But when I looked up, I saw a **monstrous** creature covered in algae, pigeon droppings, and mud.

"HELP! IT'S THE MOUSE MONSTER OF THE LAGOON!"

I shrieked.

Two seconds later I realized that I was standing in front of a giant mirror. **THE MOUSE MONSTER OF THE LAGOON WAS ME!**

Horrified, I locked the door and began to clean myself up. **1** First, I washed myself from head to tail. **2** Then, I dried myself with a paw dryer. **3** Then, I rubbed myself with scented napkins and brushed my fur with a fork. **4** And finally, I RIPPED a rose from a floral bouquet that was used to decorate the bathroom and placed it in my lapel. Only then did I smile in satisfaction.

I left the bathroom all cleaned up and feeling great. At last I could get down to business and start working on the **mystery in Venice**! Whistling a happy tune, I sat down at one of the empty tables in the café. After a while, a waiter who had been hiding behind the door came over.

"M-m-m-may I take your order?" he stammered.

I was about to respond when he whispered in my ear, "Sorry if I seem nervous. I just

saw the M-M-MOUSE M-M-MONSTER OF THE LAGOON!"

I felt awful. The poor mouse was a scampering bundle of nerves and it was all my fault! Still, I didn't want to admit that I was actually the monster. So instead I said, "Don't worry. I scared him away for good."

The waiter shot me a look of admiration and ran away. A moment later he returned with a huge plate of expensive assorted cheeses.

"This one is on the house!" he exclaimed.

"You are an incredibly brave mouse to stand up to such a **HORRIFYING MONSTER**!"

I **shook** my head. "I didn't do anything . . ." I spluttered. But he waved me off.

Leaving the café, I was bombarded by **enthusiastic** lady mice who wanted my autograph.

Suddenly, I saw a hat with pink polka dots, and long fake eyelashes. . . . **IT WAS HER! THE RODENT OF MY NIGHTMARES!**

I sprinted away as fast as my paws could carry me. I had to hide. When I spotted the most luxurious hotel in all of Venice, I went in. What else could I do?

SHARPWHISKER'S HOUSE OF GLASS

Only when I closed the door to my hotel room was I able to relax. I was finally out of danger!

I threw myself on the bed completely dressed and fell into a deep, deep sleep.

The next morning I took the first steamboat to the island of Murano. Murano is famous all over the world for its shops where GLASS and CRYSTAL are made.

I began to visit the glass factories. I examined all the store windows one by one. They were full of **COLORED** glass objects: little puppies, little fish, small horses, and wonderful families of octopuses.

But I didn't see a single GONDOLA.

Disappointed, I sat on the handrail of a bridge. I had been walking for hours. My paws **THROBBED**. My back **ached**. And even worse, I wasn't any closer to solving the **mystery in Venice!**

I must have looked pretty sad, because a young mouselet approached me. He told me his name was Twitchy, and he asked if he could help me.

"I'm looking for a crystal gondola that **lights up**, plays a little song, and is incredibly UGLY," I explained.

Twitchy burst out laughing. "My uncle makes those, but no one buys them. He makes all kinds of gondolas, and each one is more **horrendous** than the next!"

Twitchy went on. "Let's see, the last gondola he sold was about a month ago.

ONE LETS OUT A
TERRIBLE SMELL!

It was to some mouse from New Mouse City who has a stand at a flea market."

A JOLT of excitement ran through me like when you rub your paws on a furry rug and then touch something metal. ZAP! The gondola Twitchy was talking about had to be the one Petunia had bought for me at the flea market!

Twitchy led me to a WORN-DOWN shop with a window filled with gondolas, each one more awful than the one before!

But he warned me, "Don't tell my **uncle Sharpwhisker** you think his gondolas are ugly. He has anger issues."

ONE BREAKS EVERY
SINGLE PENCIL POINT!

ONE IS A PHONE WITH
AN ANNOYING RING!

ONE HAS A RADIO THAT
IS NEVER IN TUNE!

ONE CAN TELL WHEN
IT'S RAINING!

Right then a hairy paw grabbed me by the ear and pulled me into the shop.

"I'm Stuart Sharpwhisker. You're here for the apprentice position, right?" he squeaked.

I gulped. "Wh-wh-what position do you mean?" I stammered.

Sharpwhisker grabbed my snout and pulled me CLOSE to a sign on the door. "What?" he yelled. "You mean you aren't here for *this*?"

Only then did I realize what was written on the sign:

APPRENTICE WANTED

SOMEONE WHO WORKS A LOT, ACCEPTS LOW PAY, AND NEVER COMPLAINS!

It was the perfect opportunity to do my investigation and not be discovered.

"Yes, I'm here for the p-p-p-position, but . . . ," I mumbled.

"No buts, Fuzz Ball!" Sharpwhisker declared. "You're hired!"

"But . . . ," I tried again.

"You're already complaining?" he shrieked.

I quickly shook my head. There was no sense getting an angry mouse even angrier.

Still, I had wanted to tell him that I didn't know how to work with GLASS, but I never got the chance. A second later, Sharpwhisker took off his smock and hung it around my neck.

"I want FIFTY crystal gondolas by tomorrow morning!" he demanded loudly.

Then he left, **SLAMMING** the door behind him.

I took the opportunity to look around the shop. I noticed lots of trophies and medals and a photo of four gondoliers wearing shirts that read Sharpwhisker's House of Glass.

I guess old Sharpwhisker was a gondola race enthusiast.

I was still studying the photo when Twitchy finally entered the shop.

"He HIRED you?" he remarked. "Congratulations! But he'll probably fire you within two hours."

"It may be even sooner!" I sobbed. "I have no idea how to work with glass!"

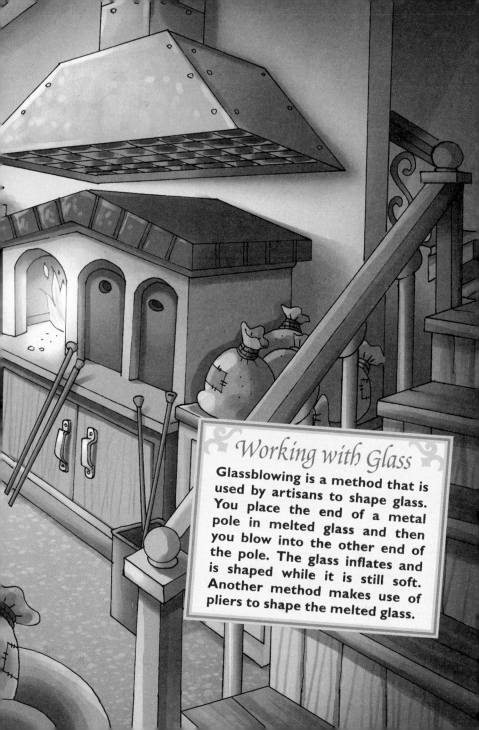

Working with Glass

Glassblowing is a method that is used by artisans to shape glass. You place the end of a metal pole in melted glass and then you blow into the other end of the pole. The glass inflates and is shaped while it is still soft. Another method makes use of pliers to shape the melted glass.

SNIFF! SIGH! SNIFF!

Twitchy explained to me how to take the glass, **SHAPE** it, and put it in the **OVEN**.

I thought I had understood everything, but as soon as Twitchy left the shop, the **PROBLEMS** started.

I **SINGED** my whiskers. . . .

I **BURNED** my tail. . . .

I **SMOKED** my snout. . . .

I singed my whiskers. . . .

I burned my tail. . . .

I smoked my snout. . .

And when I had finally managed to shape something that looked sort of like a gondola, my pieces **EXPLODED** one after the next or they **collapsed** like poorly made soufflés.

What a disaster!

WHAT A DISASTERRRRRRRRRRRRR!

My works exploded one after the next. . . .

Or they collapsed like poorly made soufflés.

In the end, a massive tower of misshapen **MELTED** glass that didn't look anything like a gondola stood in the middle of the floor.

I felt like a total failure. My whiskers **drooped** and my heart **SANK**. Oh, how had I gotten myself into such a mess? Old Sharpwhisker was going to have a fit when he saw the huge **LUMP** of glass I had created.

I pictured him chasing me with a poker

hot from the fire, and me running from him through the *twisting* streets of Venice. I'd have to keep running for the rest of my life or move to some faraway island! I'd never return to **New Mouse City** or see my beloved family again!

I was so distraught, I began to sob like a sprinkler stuck on high speed.

OH, WHY, WHY, WHY HADN'T I STAYED HOME?

Only then, between one sob and the next, did I hear that someone else was also crying.

Who could it be? Maybe it was a GHOST!

I WANT TO GO HOME!

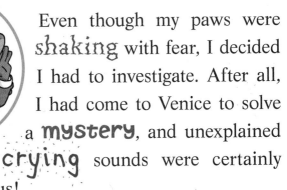

Even though my paws were shaking with fear, I decided I had to investigate. After all, I had come to Venice to solve a **mystery**, and unexplained crying sounds were certainly mysterious!

I followed the sound of the sobs and I realized they were coming from somewhere above me. Maybe there was a **secret** room! I looked everywhere until I found a **small** door. I opened it and saw a dark stairway that led to an upper level. I took a flashlight and climbed the creaking wooden stairs.

crickety creeeeak...

Meanwhile, the sobs continued: Sniff! Sigh! Sniff!

At the top of the stairs, there was another

door. I opened it and heard a **terrible** scream. . . .

"HELP! A MONSTER!"

the voice cried out.

I looked around. Hadn't I just been through a monster **SCARE**? I was all cleaned up now. How could someone mistake me for a monster again?

Then I realized I had been holding the **flashlight** under my snout, **lighting** my face up like a madmouse. **OOPS!**

I quickly turned the flashlight on the **screaming** figure, who was dressed all in white.

"HELP! A GHOST!"

I shrieked. Then I realized it was only a female mouse dressed in a white nightgown.

She looked at me in confusion.

I felt like a **fool**. I had been afraid of a mouse in pajamas! She still had tears in her eyes, so I lent her my pawkerchief.

"Sorry if I scared you," I said in a soothing voice.

THE MYSTERY OF THE CRYSTAL GONDOLA

The mouse blew her nose loudly into my pawkerchief.

HONK! HONK! HONK! Good thing I brought an extra! After she had finished, I pulled out the small note I had found in the CRYSTAL GONDOLA. Then I showed it to her.

"You wrote this, didn't you?" I guessed.

She smiled shyly.

"Yes, I don't know what I was thinking," she explained. "Who puts a message in a bottle anymore, right? I know it's a **ridiculous** idea. I guess I was just **desperate** for help and I didn't know how else to find it."

The mouse told me her name was **Hope**. I told her I had come to Venice to help her.

"That's so **sweet**," she blubbered, tears rolling down her fur. "But I'm afraid I don't know what you can do. You see, the problem is that my uncle, Stuart Sharpwhisker, won't give me permission to marry my **beloved** Arnold. Oh, Arnie . . ."

I gave her my extra pawkerchief so we both wouldn't drown in her tears.

Finally, after a few more snorts into my extra pawkerchief (too bad I hadn't brought a third!), Hope explained that Arnie was a terrible glassmaker.

"**Me too!**" I interrupted. "You should see the mess I made downstairs in the shop. . . . I think your uncle is going to fire me!"

"Probably," Hope agreed. "That's what happened to my **poor, poor** Arnie. My uncle kicked him out right on his tail! He says I can only marry a rodent who is an expert glassmaker so he can take over the business someday. It's so unfair! I love Arnie and I want to marry him!"

I nodded sympathetically as she continued.

"I locked myself up in this attic so my uncle will know how serious I am about Arnie," Hope added.

She gave me back my SOPPING pawkerchief. I coughed and felt a tickle in my nose. Did you ever notice that when you are trying not to do something, like sneeze, you sometimes feel like you can't stop it from happening?

"I promise to help you," I told Hope, wiggling my nose. "But you must promise that you will stop crying and go do something fun with your friends. Everything will be okay. . . . **AAAACHOOO!** "

At that moment I let out a sneeze so powerful it shook the room. Since I had no pawkerchief, I had to blow my nose in my sleeve. How embarrassing!

But I didn't have much time to think about it, because just then a voice thundered from downstairs.

"WHO MADE THIS MESS?"

I cringed. Old Sharpwhisker was in the house, and he sounded less than happy. Yep, even though I had solved the **mystery in Venice**, I had a **TERRiBLE** feeling my troubles were far from over.

Unfortunately, I was right. The minute I went downstairs, Sharpwhisker pointed at the lumpy pile of glass I had created.

"You're **FIRED**!" he screeched.

He probably would have thrown me out the door by my whiskers if it hadn't opened at that exact moment. The rodent who came in looked closely, with an expert air, at my misshapen pile of glass.

"What an **UNBELiEVABLE** sculpture!" he murmured. "It's a modern masterpiece! I'll buy it!"

Old Sharpwhisker charged the guy a fortune for the lump of glass.

I tried to slip away, but I was too slow. Sharpwhisker grabbed me by the ear.

"GET BACK HERE!"

he yelled.

It's a Done Deal, Fuzz Ball!

As soon as the customer left, **OLD** Sharpwhisker stuck his snout in my face. "Get to work!" he thundered. "I want twenty more of those horrible modern sculptures. Got it, **Fuzz Ball**?"

I tried to protest, but Sharpwhisker just rolled his eyes.

"I just rehired you, and already you're **COMPLAINING**?" he squeaked.

Then he began to count his money. "What a fool, throwing away all this money for a pile of junk! He could have bought three of my beautiful gondolas! But who cares? Money is more important!"

Suddenly, he looked over to the shelf of

trophies and **MEDALS** I had seen earlier. He rubbed his paws together, smiling at a photo of a gleaming gondola on the **water**. "With the money I make off your ugly creations, I can repair my beautiful gondola and win races again!" he squeaked.

But then he dissolved into tears.

Here we go again, I groaned inwardly as

Here we go again!

Waaaa!

the waterworks started. What was with this family? They all cried like **fountains**!

I passed the distraught mouse my soaked pawkerchief.

"**Now what's wrong?**" I asked him.

"Well, I have the **MONEY** to fix my gondola," Sharpwhisker said, sniffing. "But I don't have a **CREW** anymore. I fired them all. What a bunch of **complainers**. Especially that Arnold character. He was always making **cheesy eyes** at my niece. Still, it would be so great if I could win the next race. . . ."

Just then I came up with a **fabumouse** idea.

"If I can win the race for you, will you do something important for me?" I asked.

The **BIG** mouse looked me over. He touched my **puny** bicep. He stared at my

drooping shoulders and FLABBY belly.

Then he said, "You're a mess but I'm **desperate**. It's a deal, Fuzz Ball!"

He grabbed my paw and gave it a **BONE-CRUNCHING** shake.

It's a deal!

Ouch!

The minute I had agreed to the deal, I started to regret it. Why was Sharpwhisker so quick to accept my offer? Something didn't seem right, so I asked, "By the way, when is the next **gondola** race?"

I was hoping he would say it was sometime far away, like maybe **NEVER**.

Instead, he said, "It's exactly six days, fifteen hours, twelve minutes, and ten seconds from now! So you'd better start **practicing**. And you'd better not make me look like a **fool** or you'll be sorry!"

I cringed.

OH, WHY, WHY, WHY DO I ALWAYS GET MYSELF INTO THESE RIDICULOUS SITUATIONS?

Of course I didn't know the first thing about racing a **gondola**. I didn't even know how to *row*! But if I won the race for Sharpwhisker, he would have to do what I asked. And I was planning to ask him to let Hope and Arnold get *married*!

Too bad I had no chance of winning. I stuck my paws deep in my suit pockets and pulled out my cell phone. Right then I got an idea.

Quickly, I sent a text message to my friends in New Mouse City:

"SOS! Meet me at Sharpwhisker's House of Glass in Murano, Italy! GS"

Done and done.

WE'RE HERE TO HELP!

The next day at sunset, I left the shop and went to the dock where Sharpwhisker's gondola was anchored. It was an **old, peeling mess**!

Even worse, the boat was sucking in **water** like my uncle Adventure Mouse after

his three-week excursion through the desert!

Alarmed, I glanced around at the other racing boats that were docked next to Sharpwhisker's boat. Not only were they beautiful, but they were in tip-top shape!

I began to sob in desperation.

OH, WHY, WHY, WHY DO I ALWAYS GET MYSELF INTO THESE RIDICULOUS SITUATIONS?

Right then a familiar voice interrupted my crying jag.

"What's with the waterworks, Germeister? You're such a crybaby!"

I turned to find my cousin Trap laughing at me. Next to him stood my sister Thea, my nephew Benjamin, Petunia Pretty Paws, and her niece, Bugsy Wugsy.

"We're here to help, Uncle Geronimo!" squeaked Benjamin.

I was so happy to see my family and friends! I hugged everyone. Then I told them all about my ADVENTURES so far in Venice. I explained about the big race that was to be held the following Sunday and about my plan to convince Sharpwhisker to let Hope and Arnold get married.

"What a romantic story!" Petunia and Thea whispered.

Trap just rolled his eyes. "I'm getting CAVITIES with all of this gushing sweetness!" he grumbled.

A few minutes later Thea got down to business.

"Okay, everyone, there's no time to stand around shooting the cheese. We've got work to do. We've got to get in shape

for the big race!" She pulled a whistle out.
TWEET TWEET!

"We'll begin with sprints!" she squeaked.

After ten minutes, I CRASHED to the ground. Trap fell on top of me, then Benjamin, followed by Petunia and finally Bugsy Wugsy!

"**HELP!**" I squeaked from underneath the pile of mice.

Oh, what a **disaster**! If we kept going at this rate, we'd never make it to the race on Sunday!

As soon as we untangled ourselves, I turned to Thea and said in my nicest voice, "I know we need to get in shape, but before we do that, I think we should find a new **RACING** gondola. Then we can work out and practice rowing at the same time. Isn't that a great idea?"

My sister looked insulted. Did I mention she likes to be **THE BOSS** of everything?

She shot me a **LOOK**. I could tell she was about to give me a piece of her mind when suddenly a sleek gondola slipped into the canal. It was a vibrant **YELLOW**, and it was being rowed by none other than Hope Sharpwhisker!

Hope rowed up to the dock and waved.

"I heard about your plan, Geronimo, and I will do everything I can to help you win. Here, take this gondola. It was made by my

Arnold. He's an **AMAZING** carpenter," she explained.

I looked at the gondola. Hope wasn't exaggerating. Arnold truly was an amazing carpenter. It was *EXQUISITE*!

Before I could thank her, she took off down the dock. "I'm off to see my friends," she called back. "We are going to make you

I will help!

some ***fabumouse*** uniforms!"

I smiled as Hope disappeared around the corner. She was such a different mouse from the one I had met in old Sharpwhisker's attic. She had changed from a total sad sack into, well . . . someone HOPEFUL! I guess that just goes to show you how powerful **LOVE** can be!

Hi, Hope!

TWEET! TWEET!

The next week was a **NIGHTMARE**! During the day, I worked in the glass shop. In the evenings, I trained with my **family and friends**. First Thea had us run for **miles and miles**. Then she made us practice rowing for hours and hours. What a workout!

Every night I dreamed about training. I pictured myself running up an impossibly **STEEP** mountain and rowing across an impossibly **wide** ocean. The whole time I could just hear Thea's whistle blasting in my ear.

TWEET! TWEET!

I was so exhausted I could barely comb my fur in the morning. It stuck up all over the place. I was a mess! I was starting to look like the lead singer from the popular punk band **WiLD RATTiTUDES**!

Still, what could I do? I had to keep going. **Hope** was counting on me!

Unfortunately, as the day of the race approached, I grew more and more nervous. It didn't help that old Sharpwhisker continued to threaten me every day. "**You'd better not make me look like a fool or you'll be sorry!**" he would roar in my snout.

You'll be sorry!

LUCKILY, every time I started feeling scared, Benjamin and Bugsy Wugsy were there to encourage me.

"Come on, Uncle G! You can do it!" they cheered.

And **LUCKILY**, every time I wanted to skip training, Thea would show up with her trusty whistle and a pep talk.

TWEET! TWEET!

"Come on, Ger! Keep those paws moving!"

And **LUCKILY**, every time I was just feeling low, Petunia would flash me a sweet smile. Even my obnoxious cousin Trap kept me going with his **awful** jokes.

The more time passed, the stronger our team got and the **LUCKIER** I felt that I had such great family and friends!

At last it was the day of the historic regatta. I was excited and nervous at the same time.

Before the race there is a magnificent costume parade on the Grand Canal. First comes the *Bucintoro*, a luxury boat, followed by other amazing decorated boats. . . .

What an **UNBELIEVABLE** show! I was so entranced with the boats, I almost forgot about the race. But just as I began to relax, I spotted Sharpwhisker in the crowd.

Here's the Bucintoro.

The Historic Regatta of Venice

The regatta is held every year on the first Sunday of September. First held on January 10, 1315, the regatta has gained various religious, political, and military meanings through the centuries. After a historic boat procession, the races begin. The *pupparini* boats are used by young male rowers, the *mascarete* boats are used in the women's race, and the *caorline* are large river transportation boats. Finally, there is the champions' race on two-oared *gondolini* boats, which are very light and slim.

"You'd better not make me look like a **FOOL** or you'll be **SORRY**!" Sharpwhisker shrieked.

Just then the judge started the race. Immediately, my

teammates began to row as fast as they could, but my paws were petrified! I was completely frozen with **FRIGHT**!

After a few minutes, we were in last place. The crowd laughed at us. **Ha-ha-ha!**

LOVE IS A MARVELOUS THING!

Everything seemed lost until . . . something unexpected happened.

As we were floating along the Grand Canal, I suddenly spied a rodent wearing a pink polka-dot hat.

IT WAS HER! THE RODENT OF MY NIGHTMARES!

When she saw me, she began squeaking like a madmouse. "My *darling*! My **beloved**! I finally found you!"

I was horrified! Right then I felt a surge of ENERGY shoot through my body. I had to get away! I began to row so hard my paws seemed like windmills!

Over the loudsqueaker, the announcer commented enthusiastically, "And here comes the team from Sharpwhisker's House of Glass. Holey cheese, they're picking up speed! It's incredible! That yellow gondola is on fire! The crowd is going wild! Now it's down to the finish line and the winner is . . . *Sharpwhisker's House of Glass!*"

I couldn't believe it. We had WON!

"Hooray!" Benjamin and Bugsy Wugsy yelled.

Meanwhile, Petunia gave me a strange look. "Um, G, who was that lady mouse with the pink polka-dot hat?" she asked. "And why was she calling you *darling?*"

I turned PURPLE with embarrassment. "Well, um, I don't really know her . . ." I began. But before I could explain any further, we were invited to go to the platform to get

our prize. Once I was onstage, I saw a mouse with a familiar pink polka-dot hat. **IT WAS HER! THE RODENT OF MY NIGHTMARES!** She was the assistant to the master of ceremonies!

She put a **red flag** in my paws. That's the traditional prize for the historic regatta. Then she planted a kiss on my snout!

Mwah!

"You can't run anymore!" she squeaked. "I have to **kiss** the winners—that's the tradition! Plus, you said you were going to marry me, right, my little Venetian **Fuzzy Fur**?!"

Petunia frowned. "I thought you said you didn't know her, G," she said, sniffing and looking hurt.

I felt like screaming. **Oh, how, how, how do I always manage to make a mess of things?**

"I don't know her," I told Petunia. "She's been following me since I arrived in Venice, and she's got it in her head that she wants to *marry me*!"

Then I turned to my admirer. "I'm sorry, I don't want to *marry you*, miss," I explained calmly. "I'm very flattered, but I don't even know your name. Also, I'm not from Venice. I am from New Mouse City on Mouse Island."

She looked at me with disappointment.

"You're serious? You're not from Venice? Well, then you can forget it, **Fur Ball**!" she snapped.

Then she turned to Sharpwhisker and looked him over.

"And you, dear sir," she asked, "where might you be from?"

"I am **100 PERCENT** Venetian!" he responded.

Her eyes **sparkled** with excitement. "Well then, you're the rodent of my dreams!" she gushed.

Sharpwhisker **blushed** under his dark whiskers. Then he gallantly kissed her paw.

It was official. Stuart Sharpwhisker had fallen head over heels in *love*! He couldn't take his eyes off his new lady mouse, and she giggled with delight.

May I?

I decided now was the perfect time to remind him of his promise. "Um, excuse me. Sorry to bother you, but you **promised** that if I won the race, you would give me what I wanted," I said.

"Of course!" he thundered. "What do you want? Money? A house? A lifetime supply of CRYSTAL gondolas?"

I took a deep breath, gathered my **COURAGE**, and spit it out.

"No, I don't want anything for myself. I just want you to give your niece, Hope, permission to marry Arnold, the *love* of her life. And you can't make him work at the glass shop anymore. He is an amazing carpenter."

When I had finished, Sharpwhisker turned a deep shade of **red**.

I thought he would **EXPLODE**.

But instead, he SMiLED.

"Now that I know what it's like to be in *love*, I understand my niece," he said. "Love is a marvelous thing. She must follow her heart!"

I grinned. It seemed my mission in Venice was finished. Love truly is a marvelous thing!

Don't miss any of my other fabumouse adventures!

#1 Lost Treasure of the Emerald Eye

#2 The Curse of the Cheese Pyramid

#3 Cat and Mouse in a Haunted House

#4 I'm Too Fond of My Fur!

#5 Four Mice Deep in the Jungle

#6 Paws Off, Cheddarface!

#7 Red Pizzas for a Blue Count

#8 Attack of the Bandit Cats

#9 A Fabumouse Vacation for Geronimo

#10 All Because of a Cup of Coffee

#11 It's Halloween, You 'Fraidy Mouse!

#12 Merry Christmas, Geronimo!

#13 The Phantom of the Subway

#14 The Temple of the Ruby of Fire

#15 The Mona Mousa Code

#16 A Cheese-Colored Camper

#17 Watch Your Whiskers, Stilton!

#18 Shipwreck on the Pirate Islands

#19 My Name Is Stilton, Geronimo Stilton

#20 Surf's Up, Geronimo!

#21 The Wild, Wild West

#22 The Secret of Cacklefur Castle

A Christmas Tale

#23 Valentine's Day Disaster

#24 Field Trip to Niagara Falls

#25 The Search for Sunken Treasure

#26 The Mummy with No Name

#27 The Christmas Toy Factory

#28 Wedding Crasher

#29 Down and Out Down Under

#30 The Mouse Island Marathon

#31 The Mysterious Cheese Thief

Christmas Catastrophe

#32 Valley of the Giant Skeletons

#33 Geronimo and the Gold Medal Mystery

#34 Geronimo Stilton, Secret Agent

#35 A Very Merry Christmas

#36 Geronimo's Valentine

#37 The Race Across America

#38 A Fabumouse School Adventure

#39 Singing Sensation

#40 The Karate Mouse

#41 Mighty Mount Kilimanjaro

#42 The Peculiar Pumpkin Thief

#43 I'm Not a Supermouse!

#44 The Giant Diamond Robbery

#45 Save the White Whale!

#46 The Haunted Castle

#47 Run for the Hills, Geronimo!

#48 The Mystery in Venice

And coming soon!

#49 The Way of the Samurai

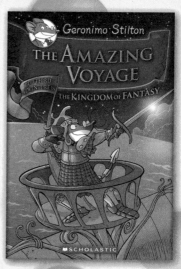

Be sure to check out these exciting Thea Sisters adventures!

THEA STILTON AND THE DRAGON'S CODE

THEA STILTON AND THE MOUNTAIN OF FIRE

THEA STILTON AND THE GHOST OF THE SHIPWRECK

THEA STILTON AND THE SECRET CITY

THEA STILTON AND THE MYSTERY IN PARIS

THEA STILTON AND THE CHERRY BLOSSOM ADVENTURE

THEA STILTON AND THE STAR CASTAWAYS

THEA STILTON: BIG TROUBLE IN THE BIG APPLE

THEA STILTON AND THE ICE TREASURE

Meet
CREEPELLA VON CACKLEFUR

I, *Geronimo Stilton*, have a lot of mouse friends, but none as **spooky** as my friend CREEPELLA VON CACKLEFUR! She is an enchanting and MYSTERIOUS mouse with a pet bat named Bitewing. YIKES! I'm a real 'fraidy mouse, but even I think CREEPELLA and her family are AWFULLY fascinating. I can't wait for you to read all about CREEPELLA in these fa-mouse-ly funny and **spectacularly spooky** tales!

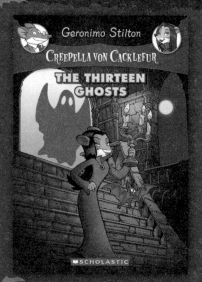

#1 THE THIRTEEN GHOSTS

#2 MEET ME IN HORRORWOOD

ABOUT THE AUTHOR

 Born in New Mouse City, Mouse Island, **GERONIMO STILTON** is Rattus Emeritus of Mousomorphic Literature and of Neo-Ratonic Comparative Philosophy. For the past twenty years, he has been running *The Rodent's Gazette*, New Mouse City's most widely read daily newspaper.

Stilton was awarded the Ratitzer Prize for his scoops on *The Curse of the Cheese Pyramid* and *The Search for Sunken Treasure*. He has also received the Andersen 2000 Prize for Personality of the Year. One of his bestsellers won the 2002 eBook Award for world's best ratlings' electronic book. His works have been published all over the globe.

In his spare time, Mr. Stilton collects antique cheese rinds and plays golf. But what he most enjoys is telling stories to his nephew Benjamin.

1. Main entrance
2. Printing presses (where the books and newspaper are printed)
3. Accounts department
4. Editorial room (where the editors, illustrators, and designers work)
5. Geronimo Stilton's office
6. Helicopter landing pad

THE RODENT'S GAZETTE

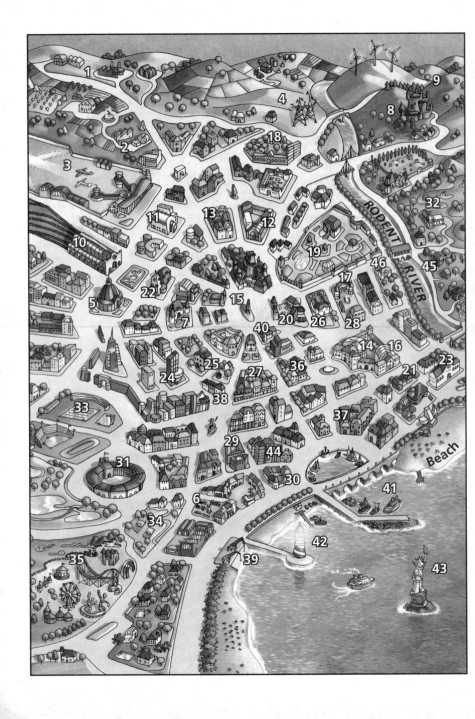

Map of New Mouse City

Map of Mouse Island

Dear mouse friends,
Thanks for reading, and farewell
till the next book.
It'll be another whisker-licking-good
adventure, and that's a promise!

Geronimo Stilton